INTRODUCTION

If you start reading or just heard about SCP and the writing community. This is the book to start reading. I put down some stories, so it is easy to begin and get into the SCP universe.

SCP means secure contain and protect. I have compiled easy to begin stories, so it is easy to start reading and learning about SCP foundation. I put it together as a book to bring more presence to the website.

Please, sit tight and enjoy the stories as it goes through the SCP universe. Tales range from mystery to horror stories. If you are looking for an inspiration or creative idea, the original website the SCP foundation has tons of authors and ideas to look through.

About SCP foundation

Mankind in its present state has been around for a quarter of a million years, yet only the last 4,000 have been of any significance.

So, what did we do for nearly 250,000 years? We huddled in caves and around small fires, fearful of the things that we didn't understand. It was more than explaining why the sun came up, it was the mystery of enormous birds with heads of men and rocks that came to life. So we called them 'gods' and 'demons', begged them to spare us, and prayed for salvation.

In time, their numbers dwindled and ours rose. The world began to make more sense when there were fewer things to fear, yet the unexplained can never truly go away, as if the universe demands the absurd and impossible.

Mankind must not go back to hiding in fear. No one else will protect us, and we must stand up for ourselves.

While the rest of mankind dwells in the light, we must stand in the darkness to fight it, contain it, and shield it from the eyes of the public, so that others may live in a sane and normal world.

TALES OF SCP

BEGINNING TO THE END

MICHAEL NOORAS

TABLE OF CONTENTS

Unfolding

In the sublevels of Site 10, Dr. Yara Mirski raised the gemstone to the light with a gloved hand, in a gesture she'd repeated a hundred times before. She admired its black contours, broken up by the mottled white pattern and the golden filigree that wrapped around its exterior.

SCP-001-Delta. The fourth SCP item considered a 'prime', or '001', item. One of several that had a hand in the creation of the Foundation. And, in Yara's opinion, by far the most frustrating.

For one, there wasn't much else to know about Delta at Level 5 clearance.

Most of the other 001 items had a great deal of falsified information attached to them, the better to confuse ever-curious researchers. Some versions were altered beyond recognition. Like Iota, Yara's favorite. Some meta-humor to give snoopers an existential crisis. Some were fabricated entirely — notably, Beta, which was a little surprising, since it was just an ordinary monster. What was so unusual or startling about that, compared to Keter cakes or Project Rho? But Beta was an invention from whole cloth; everything about it was fiction besides its ancient classification system.

Not so with Delta. Delta was strange enough on its own that people always assumed the files they had unearthed were altered. They were wrong. Delta was the most straightforward 001. A lock that appeared to literally "contain" our universe, and also something called "Apakht." It seemed like a joke from several cartoon shows, a joke made worse by the fact that it was true.

And Delta, the Lock, was still missing its Key. Not that the O5s hadn't tried to crack it open, especially the skittish ones who didn't like the idea of anyone containing anything but them. One of them had it in her head that Delta unlocked Heaven. Kept rambling on about something called the Thaumiel Initiative. It didn't matter. Not even SCP-005 could pry that lock open, and no megaton bomb could crack Delta's shell.

Yara felt the warmth of the Delta stone through her gloves, and reflected that it was perhaps fortunate that every attempt to unlock Delta had failed.

She was still reflecting on this when the first klaxon blared.

The Harbinger hated its code name.

"The Harbinger." Really. So fucking over-dramatic. They wouldn't stop using it, either. For security, they said. Harbinger. Harbinger. Harbinger? Harbinger, Harbinger,

Harbinger. It wanted to kill the son of a bitch who came up with that.

Yet... as long as it was on the premises of Site 10, it was not going to think of itself by any other identity but Harbinger. Not its name, definitely not gender. The Harbinger was an it, now, and would stay that way until this was over.

Sure, the Foundation's ability to read minds was not precisely A-grade, but considering the stakes, it wasn't planning on taking extra risk. Especially not with an 001. Especially not with Delta. The Harbinger was familiar with Delta's containment procedures, listed and unlisted, maybe too familiar... no, better not to think about that either.

The Harbinger tore through the outer containment shell around the Primary Archival Vault, wincing slightly at the ease with which the steel alloy peeled apart. The auto-defense turrets came next, followed by the chemical bath. The Harbinger's glowing white form withstood the punishment and it destroyed the turrets with a wave of its hand.

A battalion of carefully crafted containment procedures, made useless in moments. The Harbinger carefully pushed back the memories sifting up in its brain.

The Harbinger reached the Vault, the massive, aptly named octagonal prism-shaped containment chamber, custom-designed precisely for the purpose of containing SCP-001-Delta. Until now, it had done a very good job.

It was made of reinforced concrete and steel, with a time-locked access portal in the ceiling. Pretty much nothing could get through that portal.

The Harbinger grimaced. The Foundation just did not reckon with power on the right scale. That would have to change—quickly.

The Harbinger left the portal alone and ripped off the entire front side of the vault.

It walked forward two steps and stopped.

The Vault was supposed to be empty... It wasn't.

In point of fact, there was a woman sitting in it. The Harbinger recognized her. Dr. Yara Mirski. Research lead on 001-Delta.

A dangerous thought, the thought of her, bubbled up into the Harbinger's head — quickly suppressed — but it was a distraction for a key second.

Mirski was holding what appeared to be a harpoon gun on steroids, aiming it forward. She did not appear surprised to see the Harbinger, not at all—

She pulled the trigger.

God damn it, the Harbinger thought, as the bolt impaled it through the chest.

Yara Mirski hadn't known what to expect the invader, the "Harbinger", to look like, and she wasn't going to let it faze her now that she was seeing it.

But it really did look very startling.

It was shaped like a person, glowing entirely, uniformly white. She couldn't make out any features on its face. Couldn't tell whether it was male or female.

And there was something else about it — some sense about it — that felt purely otherworldly, made it hard to look at. It wasn't just the hundred wings sprouting from its back. She was reminded of the Bible stories that she'd heard in church growing up, the ones involving angels. How unwitting mortals would fall to their knees in worship, only for the angel to stop them, pull them to their feet, and rebuke them, because you should only be directing your worship to the one true living God.

There was also, of course, the harpoon in its chest, but she'd put that there. She'd almost forgotten, staring at the Harbinger's visage, until its glow started to dim and some of that intense white energy started spiraling into the harpoon.

Thank God, she thought, it's working. Then she laughed at the irony.

The Harbinger never moved its gaze from her. Only its hands moved, rising to the harpoon. She knew it couldn't remove the fully powered harpoon bolt, not while it was leeching away the being's essence. But the Harbinger didn't try.

Instead, it dismantled it. Tore open the casing, unwrapped the internal wiring, got to the power source and cracked it open with a pinch of its fingers. Immediately its light returned to full strength.

The Harbinger tossed the remnants of the now-useless harpoon aside and walked towards her. It lifted the Lock from her nerveless fingers.

Yara Mirski fell to her knees.

"Oh, cut that out," the Harbinger said. "I'm not going to kill you."

Its voice startled her back to her senses. It was mellifluous and otherworldly, still without discernible gender, but casual, undramatic. And... weary.

"Don't be too hard on yourself," it said. "Really."

She sized up the Harbinger again. No wound was visible from where the harpoon had pierced its chest. There should have been a gaping hole. There was nothing.

It didn't look at her. It was examining the Lock.

"That was very clever," it said. "It almost worked. Another time, another place... maybe it would have."

"Why didn't it?" she asked.

"If I told you that," the Harbinger said, "... well, then you'd know."

She couldn't think of a response to that.

The Harbinger reached into its form and drew from its... robes? ... the item that, somehow, Yara knew it would have. A small ornate object, resembling a key. Exactly as it had looked in the recovered sketches.

It looked so tiny. So ordinary.

"Stop," Yara said. "Wait. Please. I know you've ... You obviously want to do this. But think about it, please. Do you have any idea what could be in there? Do you know—"

"Actually..." The Harbinger seemed to chuckle a little. "I know exactly what's in there."

Yara felt a little cold. Spell of containment... "Apakht," she said.

"Apakht," the Harbinger agreed. It inserted the Key into the Lock, and turned the Key.

There was a small flash, and something about the world was irrevocably changed.

For a brief moment, the Harbinger wasn't a glowing hundred-winged angelic being. It was nothing more than an ordinary human.

Their eyes met.

"I know you," Yara said, without thinking. "You're—"

She couldn't finish the words. She couldn't even think the thought in her head. It — it — the Harbinger was doing something to stop her.

"Sorry," the Harbinger said. Its glowing radiance had returned in full. "Nothing personal." It looked at the Lock, as if watching. Or listening.

"What did you do? What is it? What did you unlock?" She could feel something vibrating in the back of her brain. Her eyes kept being drawn to the lock. It looked exactly the same, visually, but it was also incredibly different. "What's Apakht?"

"It's the End," the Harbinger said.

The fabric of reality began to unfold before their eyes.

SITE-0

Yahweh awoke in His human form in His room at Site 17, knowing that the hour had arrived.

In an instant, He was at Site 0. The personnel in the control room, some half asleep, leapt to their feet as He appeared. He took a moment to watch the dawning look of comprehension on their faces. 05-14 staggered to his feet.

"The Time has come," Yahweh intoned.

In another eye-blink, He was at the Gate. The being that the Foundation called SCP-001-Gamma bowed in front of Him, lowering its burning sword, its four flaming wings spread in reverence.

"Uriel," Yahweh said. "It is Time. Open the Gate. Lead My armies across the Earth."

"I HEAR AND OBEY, MY LORD AND MY GOD," Uriel said.

The Gate began to creak open. Behind it was an army of angels, thousands of bright creatures, many-eyed, burning with pure red light. They raised their white swords, singing a chant of war, and the rustling of countless brilliant wings filled the air.

The thing inside Site 10, the singularity that was, was not, had always been, and had never been a part of the Lock, unfurled itself like a flower.

Site 10 was demolished in an instant. No one inside had any moment for last thoughts before their deaths.

Then they were all alive again, shaken, deposited somewhere in New Hampshire. Along with Site 10, intact, aside from the destruction the Harbinger had dealt to it.

Meanwhile, the ruins of Site 10 and the corpses of everyone in it were buried deep within the vast valley that had never existed before on the planet Earth, and yet, now, had always existed, displacing a few thousand miles of desert in the Middle East. It was still both there, and not. Either way, it was.

Waves of blue and green energy washed about, and the valley filled with plants and animals the like of which had never been seen before.

In the very center, orbiting in a wash of iridescent rainbow color, the Lock hovered in the center of a tiny singularity. Open, at long last. Sending out its signal.

Dr. Everett Mann was in the middle of dissecting a recently dead instance of SCP-098 when its legs started to twitch.

Everett paused his scalpel in mid-cut and watched with curiosity. This had never happened before.

He looked over at the cage of live SCP-098 specimens. They were also acting oddly. They were stock still. Not a single red-orange limb was making so much as a twitch. SCP-098 were not exactly the calmest species of anomalous crustacean, and Everett had never seen them behave this way.

They appeared to be... watching. Waiting for something.

The dead 098 instance kept twitching.

"Hmmm," Everett said.

His cell phone vibrated in his lab coat. This was the secure cell, the one that only rang in serious emergencies. Everett put down the scalpel and picked up the call.

"Everett Mann, Site 2036, status five," he said.

"The sword falls and rises," the voice on the other line said.

"But it kills in one stroke," Everett replied.

"Emergency Order Patmos is now in effect," the voice said. "995 has breached containment. 616 has opened. We are awaiting report from 001-Gamma. We are securing 073 and 076..."

"And you want to know about 098," Everett said.

"Have SCP-098 activated?" the voice asked.

"I am sorry to disappoint you. They are acting a bit odd, but I cannot say..."

The dead 098 instance froze, then burst into pale orange flame.

After another moment passed, the other 098 specimens burst into flame, all at the same time. Little slots in their shells opened, and delicate, vibrating, dragonfly-like wings sprang out. As far as Everett could tell, each 098 instance sprouted as many wings as they had limbs. Even the dead instance. Which was now looking significantly less dead.

They breached the sides of their cage in an instant, all chittering at once in some alien language. They ripped through the plate glass window of the sealed experiment chamber and swarmed away through the site, demolishing the walls that got in their way. Everett stared after them.

"Never mind," Everett said to the voice waiting on the other line. "I'd say that probably counts."

Yahweh appeared to the entire remaining thirteen members O5 Council at once in thirteen different locations. He did not appear, of course, to the Administrator, because the last Administrator had died years ago and had not been replaced. O5-14 no longer voted on Council matters, and therefore the Council no longer need a tiebreaker vote. But to all the rest, He appeared. They were all His, and had always been His. Even the non-believers, who thought of him as nothing more than a reality bender with a god complex, would have no choice but to go along. They were all His, as sure as the hands attached to His Body.

Thirteen people leaped from their seats, from their beds, fell to their knees, tripped and fell to the ground.

"Uriel, my servant, once told your Founder to prepare for the great and terrible day of the Lord," Yahweh said in thirteen voices at once. "This day now approaches. Make your final preparations. There is nothing else you will need to do but wait. My armies ride across the Earth. Soon I will call the Four Horsemen. Once the last judgment has been unsealed, then shall the great and terrible day of the Lord come. And then all will have Paradise."

He returned to a single human body, without waiting for a reply, returned to a slight feeling of vertigo. He might have been an omnipotent super-being, but it would not have done to cram everything into this tiny human body that He'd elected to stay in until the End of Days was over. Because of that, He hadn't recently made a practice of existing in several places at once. It came naturally, like breathing, but still felt unusual, like breathing for the first time after spending long minutes underwater.

Actually, there was something odd... some little twinge of memory, triggered by what He had just done...

The thought slipped from His grasp. That was the downside of human frailty. This was a perfected human body, but even a perfected human body was still flawed compared to true omniscience.

He knew the next step, as he always knew. He would return to the ancient Valley with no name. The first place He had ever created, the precursor to Eden. The Valley where none had ever set foot but Him, and never would, not even after the End of Days.

He took a step, and was there.

And...

He wasn't alone.

Klaxons blared in Site 2036. Everett Mann listened, bemused. Emergency Order Patmos or no, there was no need for all that racket.

He stepped out of the former auxiliary research and containment chambers for SCP-098, into a mob of personnel. No one stopped to give him the time. Fairly rude, Everett thought. 098 wasn't even killing anyone. Just... leaving. The holes in the walls and ceiling could be rebuilt.

He spotted Gears in the crowd and made his way over. Another person who could be trusted to deal with situations in a reasonable fashion.

"It seems we have a massive containment breach," Gears said.

"Yes, SCP-098," Everett said. "I hear 995 and 616 have breached containment as well. 001-Gamma, soon, I'm sure. But I don't see what the fuss is about. We've stopped XK-class scenarios before, we can do it again. The only difference in this case is that we might have to deal with O5-14 putting up a fuss—"

Gears held up a hand. Interruption was not his style, Everett knew, which is partly why he could stop anyone in their tracks with that gesture. "I'm not speaking of Patmos," Gears said. "Nor 001-Gamma."

"Oh?" Everett raised an eyebrow. "What else has gotten out?"

"A whole damn lot," Gears said, perfectly calmly, swearing for the first time that Everett had ever heard.

The Gate Opens Novel by thedeadlymoose SCP / CC BY
/Original Title Modified/

http://www.scp-wiki.net/the-gate-opens

ALL BEHIND

Yahweh walked into the Valley, more astonished than He could ever remember feeling. An astonishment beyond words. He had never been at a loss for words.

The Valley — His Valley — was crowded. A massive flood of spirits, of winged things, of crawling things, of monsters, of people, of... of...

Of others.

A spirit whale swooped overhead. A gigantic furred thing lumbered its way over a distant mountain. A cadre of tiny glittering blue humanoids blew past His face, giggling, and were gone. A pure black humanoid figure appeared, blinked at Him, and vanished again. A massive not-centipede skittered by, giving Him a passing glare.

Almost in a stupor, Yahweh made His way down towards the humanoid crowd, feeling, for the first time He could remember, the instinctive need to be near others like Him.

As He approached, a figure detached itself from a crowd. A poised, brown-skinned woman with piercings in her lip, and long dark hair. For a moment Yahweh found Himself oddly attracted—

I am not a man, to wish for carnal knowledge—

"El!" the woman said.

"Who are you?" Yahweh asked, before He could register the impossibility of the question in His Head.

The woman looked at him funny. "I guess it's not surprising you don't remember. We've all forgotten a lot in the past few thousand years. But you especially."

Yahweh could think of absolutely nothing to say.

"Asherah," she said. "It's Asherah. I was your consort for several hundred years."

There were strange stirrings inside his head, alien memories that He could not comprehend—

These were other gods, they were the false idols of the
ancient times, He remembered being a god of the wind and a
god of storm and a god of the sun, a parochial, jealous deity,
He remembered creating the Heavens and the Earth in seven
days, He (he) remembered being a completely non-divine yet
unspeakably powerful boy born into suffering and pain, He
remembered being someone else forced into the shape of an
artificial god, He remembered a feeling of exultation upon
realizing He was the last god standing, the last god who had
not faded away, and the future of Earth was His forever, He
remembered having no parents, He (he) remembered his
grandmother's smile, He remembered a million impossible
contradictory memories, and they were doing it, this cursed
human form had let them in, it was them—

"Enough!" He roared.

Yahweh raised His hand, looked at the crowd of creatures
trampling through His Valley, and with a wave of His hand
wiped all the false gods out of existence.

Or... He tried to, anyway. What He actually did was wave his
hand, and then absolutely nothing happened.

"You know," Asherah said with a wry smile, "I may be your
ex, but wiping me out of existence is a really rude thing to try
to do."

She put her hand on Yahweh's shoulder without His permission, and did not explode into nothingness out of blasphemy.

"I know why you're here," she said. She pointed, directing His gaze towards the center of the Valley.

Yahweh saw it, a tiny object that floated in a rippling core of colorful light that moved like water.

It was a Lock.

"You're here to end the world," Asherah said. "And so are we. Everyone here."

"This is not possible," Yahweh said. He was feeling that vertigo again.

"To be frank," Asherah said. "I'm not actually sure I'm the Asherah, and I'm not actually sure you're the Yahweh."

"What."

"You might have noticed that you remember a whole lot of contradictory things," she said. "So do I. I remember both helping to create the world and being born into it when it was already ancient. That's just for starters. Now maybe this kind of thing is part of being a god, or maybe... Maybe it's just part of being more powerful than a human was ever meant to be." She looked back at the crowd. "Not all these things are gods, I know that for sure. We're just two of the beings that are 'supposed' to end the world. Everyone in this valley is."

Yahweh turned His glare on her. "So you — all of you — are here to make war with Me? To come against Me, to stop My End of Days?"

"Well. Yeah." She looked a little awkward, like she was trying to explain something to someone who was being painfully slow. "It's not really about you... specifically. Really, I don't think half the, uh, world-enders here knew about each other before literally a few minutes ago. They can't fight here, but... Most of them aren't happy to find out that they've got competition. Not just you."

He tried to comprehend this. A thought that He was entirely unused to having. "Do you think you can stand against the might of the one true God? Do you think you can enact your own End of Days?"

Asherah shrugged. "I don't know. Maybe? I'm not going to try."

He blinked, momentarily baffled. "You are not going to try to end the world?"

"Me?" Asherah snorted. "Fuck no."

"You told me... Then why are you here?"

"I may have been called here, but not even that Lock can make me end the world. Have you ever tried the seafood in Singapore? Have you ever used a smartphone? Run through the jungle? Seen Cirque du Soleil? Flown on an airplane? Surfed the Internet? Watched tentacle porn? Seen Star Wars? Explored the Wanderer's Library? Been lost in the concrete mazes of the new human cities? No, I like the world the way it is, thanks. It may be fucked up, but tearing it apart isn't going to improve anything."

He stared at her.

"So no," she said. "I don't plan to end the world. I actually don't plan to let you end the world either, or anyone else." She paused. "Sorry."

Divine rage rose up in Yahweh again, and He opened His mouth, only to be once again interrupted.

"Pardon me," another woman's voice said.

The new woman's voice was not raised, or powerful, but somehow everyone in the Valley heard it. And all turned to look.

She was a dark-skinned woman, African, wearing a gray suit, walking into the Valley. Her body language said she was both unassuming and confident. Yahweh knew immediately she was an ordinary human, not like these alien creatures milling around him, but He did not recognize her.

He did not recognize her.

That should not have been possible, ever, not even in this limited human form. Yahweh knew all, and even if these false gods and "world-enders" were able to stymie Him somehow, no human should—

"I come on behalf of the SCP Foundation," the woman said. "Some of you know who we are. Some of you do not. The

Foundation are the protectors of humanity. Some of you we have imprisoned, some of you we have bargained with, all in defense of humanity." She sat on the ground, cross-legged, formality inherent in her movements, some kind of ritual that Yahweh almost recognized... "I have come to talk."

There was a long silence.

"And what are you?" a crimson-skinned creature asked her.

"I am a human," she said. "I am the Administrator of the SCP Foundation."

"Impossible," Yahweh said. "I knew all the Administrators. The last one died years ago, and you are not he. You are none of them."

"I'm protected from—" the woman started.

"You are not human," a panther-shaped entity shouted from the crowd. Yahweh seethed at the interruption. "If you were human, we would be able to touch you."

"I am protected," the Administrator said again. "But outside of my protection, I really am nothing more than a human. Like all the humans you plan to kill in your quest to end the world."

"Then what do you want, Human?" another world-ender asked.

"We can open the way to worlds free of sentient life. Many worlds. Enough room for all of you. You won't have to end this world. No humans will have to die. You will have a hundred others." She paused. "I want you to let this world live out the rest of its history in peace."

A clamor of voices broke out. Not all of it was verbal - much was broadcast by thought.

What are you saying—

Is this supposed to be an insult—

I come to save the world, I must end it to save it—

This is not a human's place—

This is the end of days—

How did you come here, how did any of you—

All will burn—

This age is over, as the ages before it also had an end—

Who will deny me, certainly not a tiny thing like—

"What do you offer in exchange, Human?" a massive, fox-furred being asked, once the voices started to quiet down.

"In exchange..." The Administrator hesitated. Though He could not read her mind, Yahweh could tell that she was unsure about what she was about to say. Uncertain, even afraid.

"In exchange, we will not destroy you."

Silence. A few of the entities laughed. Most looked uncaring or simply baffled. Many began to move on, apparently losing interest.

"Will none of you consider my offer?" the Administrator asked.

No one answered.

"Very well." The Administrator drew herself up.

"Why do you not join us, Human?" an amorphous blue form called out from the crowd. "Take your Foundation and come end the world with us. In the new world, you will have anything you could wish for. Anything you could imagine."

"We are the Foundation," the Administrator said. "We will not worship you. We will not join you. We will not go back to hiding in fear of you. I hope you will change your minds, but we will stand against you, and alone, if we have to."

She looked at Yahweh, directly, and for a fleeting instant, Yahweh thought of Himself as SCP-343.

"All of you," the Administrator said.

Her form flickered, and she vanished from the Valley, leaving no trace behind.

BEGINNING TO THE END

The intruder appears to her as she kneels on a sloping, angular plane, of waving, waist-high red grass. Her field notebooks flutter, their pages fan back, and the grass is blown back in concentric circles. The thing itself is awash in glow and flickering shadows, then drops like a bird onto the firmament.

"YOU," it says. "What the hell are you doing here?"

"Testing out early retirement options," says the woman in the grass, who hasn't looked up yet. She's petite, pale, with a ropy build. A scar running down her face. "There's lots of area for phylogenetic research, in the-"

"Oh sweet Cthulhu. No you're not," the intruder snaps. "For one, you're still, like, a hundred years younger than Garrison. You're not retiring now. And whatever's going on, you're going to have to get over it, soon. We have business. Your whole world-"

"You know..." The woman picks herself up, and dusts off the knees of her incongruous lab coat. The red blades of grass stand up on end, and the intruder can finally see clawed footprints in the muck underneath them. "I know I'm dreaming right now. And for part of my subconscious, you're being very demanding."

She turns around, slowly. Then she notices his suit and bowler hat.

"Oh," says Sophia Light.

"Right," says 990.

Sophia looks around. "I would have cleaned up the place if I knew you were coming," she says. "Why are you here?"

"Well, I'd say we're due for a little calamity. Wouldn't you?" He holds out his hand. "I've been blindsided, as of late. What I once saw in the future is no longer there at all. Something has changed. Big things are moving, Doctor Light. Whole lot of fish, no time to fry. Your whole world is about to turn sideways. Need to see?"

She touches his hand, and their surroundings change. Halfway-outdated Foundation architecture, older site, probably an auxiliary wing. Not one she's been in, in some time anyways, but the feel of it seems familiar. They are several stories underground, but sunlight streams in from gaping holes ripped out above them.

"This, Doctor, is your precious Site Fourteen."

"Is it?" She tilts her head all around, pursed her lips. "Was Agent-"

"Ordinarily, I'd care, but right now this goes beyond your personal crap. And you're going to sit back and listen to what I say. It's not just Fourteen. It's going to be all of them. Something's changed and I can't tell you exactly how it'll play out, but your precious Foundation is about to be horribly, hideously, calamitously outmatched."

The echoey, almost-silence of the burned-out building is, if you listen hard enough, rather calming.

"How can I stop it?"

"No one can stop it."

Sophia looks up, and studies his face. "You just said you've been blindsided by this nonspecific disaster. And I haven't heard Johanna or the fivers or anyone getting a visit, so you haven't been working down the ladder. So what, this is a social call?" She pauses. "And how do you know it's unstoppable?"

He glares at her. "If this seems unplanned, I didn't expect you to work that out in your sleep, but fine- yes, it is, I've been low on time. But listen. Here's what you would have done, if I weren't here. You would have looked at the information. Talked it over with Garrison and Barculo and Vaux, whoever you trust these days. Maybe phoned a friend. Then, you would have compared what's happening with previous disasters of similar magnitude, looked for anomalous causes, then, finally, began preparing for the worst plausible result you could extrapolate."

"That's what I would have done?"

"Yes. It would have been smart."

"And what are you saying I should do?"

"I'm saying that this is going to get worse, and if you want to even live to have a battle plan, you're going to prepare for the worst- to start. Find your resources, gather your armies. Might play out that not everyone in the Foundation is your best friend."

She nearly laughs. "What armies?"

"See, that kind of attitude is going to have to change." 990 flickers in place, like a movie still. He checks his watch.

"I mean," says Sophia, and then she does laugh. "I think you think you're doing me a favor. So thanks for telling me about the impending doom and all that jazz. But this is hilariously nonspecific. Can you tell me, say, what's going to happen? Or what kind of 'preparations' I should make?"

The bowler-hatted figure in his outdated suit checks his watch once more. "No, I can't, and it's already happened. Welcome to Armageddon. This is Day One." He flickers again, and starts to walk away, then pauses. "Oh, and you're right- I'm not working down the ladder, and I am doing you a favor. Whenever you get done... Remember that."

She blinks. "You think somehow I'll help you-"

And then he is gone. Sophia is alone in the skeletal ruins of Site 14. Motes of dust seep gently down from the surface, landing on the illuminated surface of an unreadable Object Class designation, bolted to the remains of a metal door. Deep in the fallen timber and rebar, something begins to stir.

Sophia sat bolt upright. Someone was pounding on her door. She dimly registered darkness, the scent of cleaning fluid, the tight sensation of hospital corners on fitted sheets. Her phone ringing and ringing. Knocking harder.

She pulled herself out of bed instantly, nearly falling as the blood in her legs caught up to her head, then gathering herself to pull the door open. "Yes?"

Elliot Barculo, Regional Security Director, currently stationed at the Svalbard Site, was propped in her doorway. Deep lines in his face. "Jesus Christ, Sophia, were you asleep?"

"I- maybe-" She squinted, confused, and rubbed her eyes. The idea of Sophia Light oversleeping was preposterous- "Did something happen at Site 14?"

He scowled. "How the hell did you know that?"

Oh.

"It's not just Site 14. Oh Christ." Barculo sighed and turned his back. "No time. Johanna's waiting in the debrief room. Plane's in the airfield, if the sky's safe. We need a plan. Come on."

Sophia grabbed her jacket, and closed the bedroom door behind her. "Start talking on the way."

Johanna Garrison, perched on the end of the conference table, looked older than Light could have ever imagined. Gabriel Bryant, personnel and espionage director, stood behind Johanna with an arm on her shoulder. Johanna and Sophia shared a look as Sophia entered the room, but neither said anything about the timing. Sophia's friend and apprentice, Charles Vaux, fixed an apprehensive look at her. Alerts were streaming onto Sophia's phone- containment breached at sites 14, 16, 19, 23, 40, 41, 42 A through D.

"This started at Site 10?" Sophia asked.

"As best anyone can figure," said Bryant. "The site itself actually suffered no damage, although it teleported entirely to New Hampshire shortly before the other breaches."

"New Hampshire?"

"Right. Researcher there- Dr. Yara Mirski- claims to have made contact with the responsible entity, says she tried to stop it."

"What was the entity?"

"Actually, we have no idea."

More than a handful of breakouts, sites around the world reported anomalies and disturbances. On the conference room screen, a report came in that SCP-1688 had materialized over its containment area and grown to four times the size it had ever been, driving arrows of lightning all over a nearby Foundation facility and small town. Reportedly the whole town had unilaterally joined together, in some kind of engineering project on a massive scale. At the same time, a ring-shaped stormcloud had formed several kilometers to the east, and was raising pallid spirits from the ground that it passed over. Reports showed SCP-460 moving across the sky at impossible speeds, with an army of ghosts trailing in its wake.

The next update was only video: a lightning storm, massive and striking ground so frequently that it looked like a comb of jagged white lines, and a large, circular, ochre stormcloud, rammed halfway into it. Faint white figures on the ground below seemed fixed in place, or spun out of shape like molten glass.

Ten minutes later, the yellow cloud and the ghosts were gone completely, and the lightning was still going.

"Okay." Sophia stopped pacing, and panned through incoming alerts. "The O5 Council has been silent, which makes me think we've been attacked. CI? Maybe the Hand? A lot of the missing ones are Sentients. The other anomalies could be... distractions?"

"But not all. For heaven's sake, Sophia, the duck pond?" Garrison was still staring at the screens.

"Putting something there is the kind of mistake I'd make if I was trying to get at us with an incomplete set of archives." Sophia's phone rang, despite the fact that she'd disabled it. She looked at the caller.

"Light," Barculo said in monotone, "I know that some of these sites are yours, and you have to get to stabilizing, but some are mine too, and we need to start tracking them down. I don't think they're going to the same place, but there must be a link, so we'll start pulling-"

"Actually," said Sophia, "I'm going to start planning for a second wave, possibly worse than this one. I would start now. And I'm sorry, I have to take this."

She stepped out of the conference room. All down the hall, LEDs on security cameras and recorders were going out.

Then she picked up the phone, and let it sit between her hand and her ear, and inhaled for a moment before speaking.

"Are you really her?" she asked.

"Yes," said the Administrator of the SCP Foundation. "SCP-027, I think, is about to break containment." Fingers clacked on a computer keyboard. "As it's your site, please do anything humanly possible to prevent this from happening."

"Of course," said Sophia automatically.

The call quit.

She started dialing.

Ragnarok

They came from beyond the world, from over the world, from under the world. They came from inside the stars and from behind the rain. They came from the known lands and they came from the secret places of old.

The vast ones who drank of the nebulae, the small ones who did not care what happened beyond the banks of their rivers, the ones who bathed in the light and the ones who watched from the shadows, the ones who loved us and the ones who forgot about us, the ones who hate us now and the ones who love us still, the ones who sung with the rats and the ones who swam with the leviathans, they came from far and near, they came one and all. They came to end the world.

The machine labeled SCP-720 put the last finishing touches on the final model planet in its most recent solar array. It trained its claw upward, as if looking once more, wistfully, to the stars.

SCP-720 had no name, no thoughts the way humans would account for thoughts, and certainly no internal mechanism for vision. But you would have to say that it could 'see' nonetheless, for what else could you call what it did when it directed its mechanical parts towards the sky?

Either way, this time, SCP-720 'saw' something different. Something prowling between the beautiful orbs and masses of color... something looking towards Earth. Looking back towards SCP-720.

A sea of glimmering eyes.

Words formed in the not-mind of SCP-720.

Today is the day your prayers will be answered.

A long moment passed, and then a single other word formed in the not-mind of SCP-720, and vibrated there for a long time.

Awaken.

And so it did.

What appeared to be a vast wall of fur approached the Earth, sank through the sky, and landed on the ground, to find everything it had loved gone. Her fellow gods were on their way, but as always, she had arrived first, a mother eager to be reunited at long last with her children, now that the time of the end had come.

She had been gone for thousands and thousands of years. She had gone as her children had first looked to the stars, and it was then that she had known that they would be alright.

And now there was no trace of them.

Their beautiful webbed cities, their songs that had filled the planet with joy, their vast works of art to stun even a god's eye - gone. All gone. All that remained were their bones, and living on top of them, the hairless apes that they had once kept in zoos with other animals, now risen to dominate the planet. And they did not even remember her children. They moved through their lives like ants, building their wooden and metal hives over the graves of her greatest loves. This was sacred ground they defiled, and they did not know or care.

Ur-An-Uum raised her head to the sky and cried a rending wail of anguish.

She mourned for a long time, a noise heard on high, her wails causing earthquakes and tsunamis across the planet, weeping for her children. She did not quell her sorrow. The only things left to die from her pain were the furless apes.

This was to be a time of joy, but there was only sorrow left. She would not be comforted, for her children were no more.

And then...

She felt something. The tiniest glimmer in her mind.

And she felt hope.

Ur-An-Uum called out for her children, the creatures that she now knew the furless apes called a sea of derogatory names, the least insulting of which was "SCP-1000".

Her children answered.

The entity awoke with a start, not knowing where it was, or, on reflection, who it was. All it knew was that The Time Had Come.

It rose from its grave, shattering a mountain as it did so, and hurtled itself into the atmosphere, trying to get its bearings.

The entity gazed across the world. Everything was different. Humans - they were everywhere. Not just scattered here and there across the great expanses, but living in massive villages, villages the likes of which the entity had never seen.

Not that it was complaining. Humans had fed it well with their worship and blood sacrifices in the olden days. Now that there were so many more humans, why, the entity would certainly soon be satiated beyond compare.

This was fortunate, because it had been asleep a very long time, and it was very hungry.

The entity cast about for a place of power. And found far too many. Far more than there had ever been before. It did not understand what to make of this knowledge, but, again, it did not complain. It only needed to pick one place of power for now, a simple one, to give it initial shape again. It chose the nearest one. A "Foundation Containment Site". Yes, this would certainly do. The humans had already invested this place with much of their energy. It must be a sacred place to them. An Es See Pee, they called it.

The entity would dine well indeed.

It wasted no more time, but hurtled directly into the place of power - a body of water, it saw - and landed inside it with a massive impact. It drank in the place of power and everything in it - the water, the local wildlife, the human-made metalworkings and detritus - and took the shape of a massive titan be-straddling the countryside. Man-shaped, so that the humans would understand the form to which they would soon direct their hearts and their prayers and their blood and their pleadings for mercy.

The eldritch entity that had merged with SCP-765 opened its mouth.

"QUACK," it said, its voice reverberating across the land.

First the rooster of crimson crowed, then the rooster of gold, then the rooster of soot-red.

A bloodstained watchdog bayed in its cave. Its eons-old bindings broke, and it ran free.

The sound of a great trumpet echoed across the Earth, with no apparent source. People stopped in the streets in New York, Delhi, London, Cape Town, and listened in confusion.

The Midgard serpent Jörmungandr stirred in its slumber. The shifting of its form caused tsunamis along several coastlines, demolished a number of villages in Greenland. A massive wolf, visible from hundreds of miles away, stalked across Denmark, accompanied by an army of burning giants.

Ragnarok had come.

The Administrator swung around in her chair to face the man who had just entered the room behind her.

"You knew I was coming," the man said. "You let me in."

"Yes," said the Administrator.

"You know you're dreaming, I'm sure," the man said. "And of course... you also know who I am."

"SCP-990," the Administrator said. She looks at him again. The suit, the bowler hat... or was that a fedora? "Nobody," she said. "But most importantly..." She picked up a file folder on her desk. "The first Administrator."

The two Administrators looked at one another.

"I saw you in the crowd in the Valley," the current Administrator said. "I knew to expect it, but... tell me it isn't true."

"I'm sorry," the first Administrator said. "It's true."

"This betrays everything we stand for," the current Administrator said. "You said it once yourself. We secure. We contain. We protect. We keep humanity out of the dark. For you to become one of these things..."

"I also said that the Foundation must stand in the dark, so that humanity could live in the light." The first Administrator hesitated. "Please believe me, if there had been any other choice to make, I would have made it. This has to be done. I hope you'll see why, soon." He hesitates. "I came here hoping to recruit you, you know. You and yours. I am sorry that I cannot tell you more, but I hope you will consider my offer."

"Tell me something," the current Administrator said. "This 'Harbinger'. Who are they?"

"I don't know," the first Administrator said. "It's true that I anticipated this for a long time, but... this chain of events blindsided me too."

"I know it's one of yours." The current Administrator's voice sounded impatient for the first time. "Who is it? Someone loyal to you, of course. Only someone with level 5 clearance could have pulled this off, so that does narrow the list down. Charles Gears? Jack Bright? Alto Clef? Kain Pathos Crow?" She paused. "I know it's not Sophia Light. Frederick Williams? Chelsea Elliot? Hell, Simon Glass?"

"I sincerely do not know," the first Administrator said. "Listen. The O5 Council is already compromised. SCP-343. And... well, you know the rest. I've cut off their communications, but they won't wait long to move. We should be in this together."

"I agree," the current Administrator said. "I know enough to know you don't have to do this. You'll have a compulsion, but I'm told it's minor. Easily overcome. Perhaps will not even return."

"The world must end," the first Administrator said. "Help me end it in the only way the Foundation — the only way humanity — will come out on top. There are more world-enders coming. You already know that dozens are already awake, and that hundreds soon will be. More and more will be waking up, the longer the Lock is open. And worse, more will arrive. The ones not already on Earth. This is the only way forward we have."

"Then we do not have anything left to say to each other," the current Administrator said.

"I am truly sorry to hear that," the first Administrator said.

"As I am truly sorry to say it," the current Administrator said.

The two Administrators nodded at each other, respectfully, and turned away from each other.

The first Administrator walked away and dissolved into the dreamscape. The current Administrator turned back to her dream-desk and waited for the sedative she'd taken to wear off.

Then she woke up, and got to work.

ORIGINAL CREDITS

Original Titles listed with origin websites.

#1

"Apakht" Novel by thedeadlymoose SCP / CC BY /Original Title Modified and contents/

http://www.scp-wiki.net/apakht

#2

The Gate Opens Novel by thedeadlymoose SCP / CC BY /Original Title Modified/

http://www.scp-wiki.net/the-gate-opens

#3

Revelation Novel by SCP / CC BY /Original Title and contents Modified/

http://www.scp-wiki.net/revelation

#4

Storm Front by Sophia Light SCP / CC BY /Original Title Modified/

http://www.scp-wiki.net/stormfront

#5

Awakenings Novel by thedeadlymoose SCP / CC BY /Original Title Modified

http://www.scp-wiki.net/awakenings

OTHER SCP SHORT STORY BOOKS

Tales of SCP Book of Horror stories (edition 1)

Tales Of SCP book of horror stories include the top rated tales from SCP foundation.

Tales Of SCP Short Horror Stories edition 1 book 2

This book is about the thrilling and interesting story of SCP 231.

Made in the USA
Monee, IL
26 January 2021